WORLD WAR I

BY THOMAS K. ADAMSON

The Child's World

Published by The Child's World®
1980 Lookout Drive • Mankato, MN 56003-1705
800-599-READ • www.childsworld.com

ACKNOWLEDGMENTS
The Child's World®: Mary Berendes, Publishing Director
Red Line Editorial: Editorial direction
The Design Lab: Design
Amnet: Production
Content Consultant: Jason Myers, Faculty/Staff Support Spe-
cialist & Operations Coordinator, University of Denver

Photographs ©: Bettmann/Corbis/AP Images, cover; AP
Images, 5; Harris & Ewing/Library of Congress, 7, 18; Bet-
tmann/Corbis, 9, 27; Bain News Service/Library of Congress,
10, 12, 28; Realistic Travels/Library of Congress, 11; Library
of Congress, 14, 22; Keystone View Company/Library of Congress, 15; Berliner Verlag/Corbis, 16; Corbis, 19, 24; James
Montgomery Flagg/Library of Congress, 21

Design Element: Shutterstock Images

ISBN 9781631437083
LCCN 2014945406

Printed in the United States of America
Mankato, MN
November, 2014
PA02243

ABOUT THE AUTHOR

Thomas K. Adamson has written dozens of nonfiction books for kids on sports, space, history, math, and more. He lives in Sioux Falls, South Dakota, with his wife and two sons. He enjoys sports, card games, and reading and playing ball with his sons.

TABLE OF CONTENTS

CHAPTER ONE

WOUNDED IN THE WOODS

★ ★ ★

On June 6, 1918, Floyd Gibbons walked into Belleau Wood in northern France. Gibbons was a writer for a Chicago, Illinois, newspaper. He was there to write about American Marines. They were fighting in what some called "The War to End All Wars."

The terrible war had dragged on for almost four years. In 1914, Germany had invaded France. The United States joined the war in 1917 to help France and its **ally** Great Britain. They were called the Allies. The Allies fought the Central Powers, which were Germany and Austria-Hungary. In May 1918, American soldiers were in their first big battle of the war.

Many countries, like Spain and Switzerland, remained officially neutral during World War I. ▶

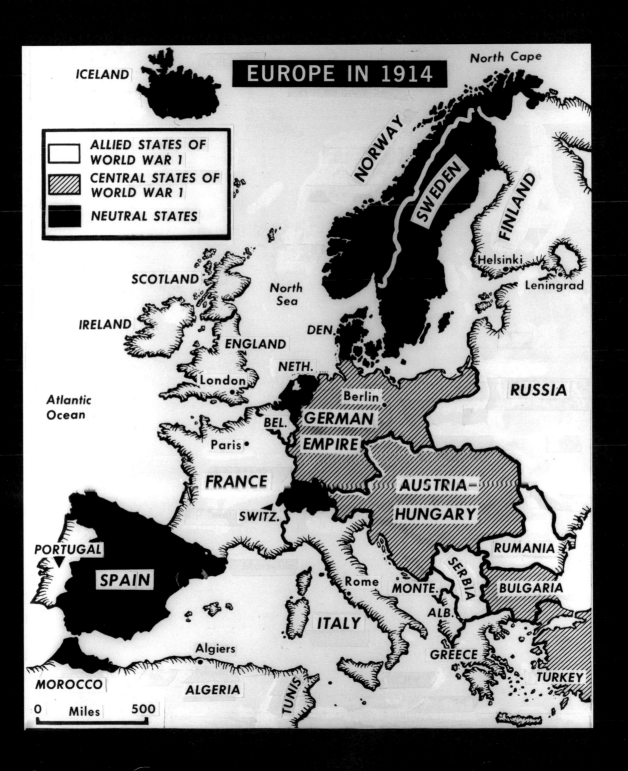

EUROPE IN 1914

ICELAND

ALLIED STATES OF WORLD WAR 1

CENTRAL STATES OF WORLD WAR 1

NEUTRAL STATES

North Cape

NORWAY

SWEDEN

FINLAND

Helsinki

Leningrad

SCOTLAND

North Sea

IRELAND

DEN.

ENGLAND

Atlantic Ocean

London

NETH.

Berlin

RUSSIA

BEL.

GERMAN EMPIRE

Paris

FRANCE

SWITZ.

AUSTRIA-HUNGARY

PORTUGAL

SPAIN

Rome

MONTE.

SERBIA

RUMANIA

BULGARIA

ALB.

ITALY

Algiers

GREECE

TURKEY

MOROCCO

ALGERIA

TUNIS

0   Miles   500

5

U.S. Marines led an attack on the Germans in Belleau Wood. Gibbons followed the Marines as they marched across a field. With no warning, machine gun fire erupted from the woods. The Marines flattened themselves on the ground. So did Gibbons. German soldiers sprayed them with bullets.

Gibbons tried to crawl away. He felt something burn his left arm. A bullet had hit him just above the elbow. He pushed himself forward. Another bullet hit him in the shoulder. He still inched forward.

A third bullet hit Gibbons. This one bounced off a rock. It hit him in the left eye and came out the right side of his head. Gibbons saw everything go bright white for a moment. He wondered if he was dead.

Gibbons wasn't dead. But his face was bleeding badly. He had to stay low to avoid the German machine gun fire.

Gibbons waited three hours for it to get dark. He then crawled to the woods. A U.S. soldier helped Gibbons walk down a road. After about a mile, they found other

COMMUNICATION

During World War I, radios were too heavy to carry around in battle. Telephones were unreliable. Phone lines were often broken during combat. Carrier pigeons could bring messages to specific locations. Some pigeons even received medals for bravery.

wounded men being treated by doctors. Gibbons was eventually brought to a hospital near Paris.

He lost his eye. But he was still able to write. He wrote a book about his experience in the war.

It took three more weeks for the U.S. Marines to win the battle in Belleau Wood. With U.S. help, the Allies would soon defeat the Central Powers.

Floyd Gibbons recovered after being wounded in Belleau Wood.

Many of the soldiers in World War I entered the military through the draft. In the draft, men are chosen randomly to join the military. Imagine if you were sent thousands of miles away to fight in a war. How would you feel having no choice whether or not to fight?

CAUSES OF THE WAR

★ ★ ★

World War I was a complex and brutal war. It all started in Eastern Europe with an assassination.

Archduke Franz Ferdinand was next in line to be emperor of Austria-Hungary. Austria-Hungary was a European country bordering Germany, Russia, and several other countries. On June 28, 1914, he visited Sarajevo in Bosnia. Austria-Hungary had recently taken over Bosnia. Bosnia was populated largely by an ethnic group called the Serbs. Many Serbs wanted Bosnia to be free from Austrian rule. They wanted to rule the country where they lived.

Ferdinand and his wife Sophie rode down the street in a car with no roof. The driver took a wrong turn. He stopped to turn around. A Serbian **nationalist** named Gavrilo Princip stepped up to the car. He pulled out a gun and fired twice. One bullet hit Ferdinand and the other hit Sophie. They both died within minutes.

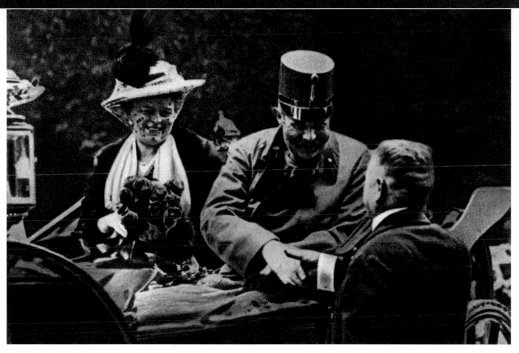

Archduke Ferdinand (center) with his wife in Sarajevo one hour before Gavrilo Princip killed them.

Serbian nationalists thought killing Ferdinand would help free Bosnia from Austrian rule. Instead, it set into motion events that would change world history.

Austria-Hungary wanted to attack the country of Serbia in response to the murder, since Serbian leaders were thought to have been involved in the assassination. But Austria-Hungary knew Serbia's ally Russia would help defend the Serbs. Germany said it would support Austria-Hungary. Germany wanted more power in Europe. Helping Austria-Hungary was an opportunity for Germany to seize that power.

German soldiers in Belgium travel to the front.

Serbia moved its army to defend itself. Austria-Hungary did the same. Russia began preparing for war.

France would not agree to remain neutral in the war, so Germany declared war on it. Since the mid-1800s, German military leaders had a plan for fighting a war on two fronts. They would invade France, to the west, as quickly as possible. Then they would turn to the east and fight Russia.

On August 4, 1914, Germany put the plan into action. It invaded Belgium on the way to France. Germany sent 750,000 men across the border. Britain joined the war to help Belgium and France. Britain had signed a **treaty** that said it would defend Belgium if that country was attacked. Civilians in Belgium had to flee. Many were killed.

British soldiers in a trench take enemy fire.

The German army then stormed into France, making it as far as the French capital, Paris. However, the French put up a stronger resistance than the Germans expected. The Germans retreated from Paris but still held much of northeastern France. Both sides dug **trenches** to try to hold territory. For the next four years, the patterns of these trenches stayed almost the same. The lines of trenches stretched from the coast of the North Sea to Switzerland.

The front trench was protected with barbed wire and large guns. The area between the two armies' trenches was called "no man's land." Usually, anyone trying to cross no man's land was quickly killed.

German soldiers operate a machine gun during World War I.

Trench warfare meant neither side could win easily. The two sides were at a **stalemate**. The Great War had begun.

While the German army marched into Belgium and France, Russia attacked Germany on its eastern border. Germany now had to send soldiers to the Eastern Front to fight Russia. Russia gained ground, but Germany fought the Russian army back. Russia also attacked Germany's ally Austria-Hungary.

At the same time, Austria-Hungary tried invading Serbia. The Serbs were fiercely patriotic. They drove Austria-Hungary back. The Serbs were even able to cross briefly into Austria. The Austrians lost thousands of soldiers in these battles.

Germany tried to help Austria-Hungary. The German armies were already stretched thin. They tried to battle in several places at once.

The war soon became a world war. Germany and Britain had territory all over the world. Countries near those places felt threatened. Japan attacked German territory in the Pacific Ocean and China. Germany attacked the British colony of South Africa. In fall 1914, the war expanded to the Middle East. There, Britain backed a revolt against the Turkish Ottoman Empire, a German ally.

Soldiers in WWI had more powerful weapons than in earlier wars. Machine guns could kill far more quickly than guns of the past. They could fire 600 bullets per minute. Large guns had long range. This made trench warfare even more deadly.

CONDITIONS IN THE TRENCHES

The trenches were a terrifying place to be in the war. Trenches sometimes filled with rain and mud. Rats ran freely in the trenches. They ruined food and ran across the men as they tried to sleep. Shells exploded nearby constantly. The soldiers thought they could be hit any minute.

U.S. soldiers put on their gas masks.

The Germans introduced poison gas to the war in April 1915. Germans first used chlorine gas. This gas makes the victims' lungs fill with fluid. Another gas used was mustard gas. Both the Central Powers and the Allies used it. Mustard gas could be fired in a **shell** from a distance. Mustard gas burned soldiers' skin, eyes, and even their lungs when they breathed it in. It did not always kill. It polluted the area where it landed for weeks. Many veterans of the war had breathing problems for the rest of their lives.

Soldiers carried gas masks. They even needed masks to protect themselves from their own attacks. The wind could

American soldiers go "over the top" of the trench into no-man's-land.

carry chlorine gas back at the attackers. Gas masks were even made for horses.

ANOTHER VIEW

Leaving the trench to attack the enemy was called going "over the top." Such an attack meant almost certain death or injury. How would you feel as a soldier if you were ordered to jump out of the trenches?

German troops march through a cloud of dust on their way to the trenches during the Battle of Verdun.

Planes were still a new invention at the time of World War I. They observed enemy movements. Planes had machine guns for aerial combat. Planes also dropped bombs.

Throughout 1915, the Allies launched several attacks against Germany. They wanted to win back territory in France and Belgium. Thousands of soldiers were killed in these attacks. Neither side could achieve a real victory.

In February 1916, the French and Germans battled near the small town of Verdun in northern France. The Battle of Verdun would be the longest and bloodiest battle of the war.

From February to July, 20 million shells were fired in the battle zone. The landscape was charred. Forests were cleared. Nearby villages were wiped out. Approximately 500,000 men were killed and wounded in this long battle. The fighting continued through the summer and stopped by fall. But another horrible battle had already begun nearby.

On July 1, the British army launched a major attack against German forces near the Somme River north of Verdun. The Allies were trying to break the stalemate.

The attack began with a week's worth of shelling on the German trenches. Then 100,000 men entered no man's land.

However, the shelling did not damage the German dugouts. Worse yet, the barbed wire in front of the German positions was still in place. The British leaders did not realize this. When the British soldiers entered no man's land, 20,000 were killed. It was the highest death toll in a single day of the war.

The First Battle of the Somme dragged on for four months. More than one million men ended up dead or wounded. Again, no one could claim victory.

CHAPTER THREE

THE UNITED STATES ENTERS THE WAR

★ ★ ★

The war seemed distant to Americans. President Woodrow Wilson insisted on keeping the United States **neutral**. Most agreed with him.

This view started to change. On May 7, 1915, a German submarine called a U-boat torpedoed the passenger ship *Lusitania*. The ship sank in 15 minutes. Of the more than 1,100 people on the ship who died, 128 were Americans. This attack angered Americans and put pressure on Wilson to do something.

Woodrow Wilson

A German U-boat surfaces during World War I.

By 1916, Germany was running out of food. British ships prevented shipments from getting to Germany. Germany decided to attack civilian ships without warning. They had avoided that since the sinking of the *Lusitania*. They wanted to avoid angering the United States. But now the Germans thought sinking British ships was more important because Great Britain had such a powerful navy.

In early 1917, Britain intercepted a telegram that German foreign minister Arthur Zimmerman sent to Mexico. The message promised Mexico the land they had lost to the United States in past wars if Mexico became Germany's ally. The captured message made big news in the United States and angered Americans even more.

The United States had now been directly threatened. And Germany's submarine attacks were killing Americans. Wilson was convinced that the United States could no longer remain neutral. He asked Congress to declare war on Germany. Congress declared war on April 6, 1917.

The U.S. government quickly worked to get Americans to support the war effort. Songwriters were hired to write patriotic songs. The songs encouraged men to sign up for the war. Popular songs like "Over There" gave people confidence that the United States would help finish the war with a victory.

A recruiting poster showed an authoritative, almost angry Uncle Sam pointing his finger. It had the words "I Want You for U.S. Army" across the bottom. The poster was seen everywhere. Four million of these posters were printed in 1917.

The famous "Uncle Sam" poster recruited many young men for the U.S. military.

Vladimir Lenin

Because of the shortage of food in Europe, the American government encouraged people to waste less food. The government promoted Meatless Mondays. People also planted victory gardens. They grew their own vegetables so that more could be sent to Europe. Such activities allowed the United States to avoid food **rationing.**

By early 1917, Russia was suffering from food shortages. Soldiers were becoming unwilling to keep fighting. Russian casualties were high, and the Russian people could not tolerate it any longer.

On March 2, 1917, the Russian tsar, or monarch, agreed to give up power. In November, a new government took over, led by Vladimir Lenin. Russia and Germany agreed to a

BLACK REGIMENTS IN THE WAR

During World War I, the U.S. Army was segregated by race. Four black regiments fought with the French. The entire 369th Division was awarded the Croix de Guerre medal for bravery under fire.

three-month **armistice**. This ended Russia's role in World War I. Russia had to give land to Germany.

This was followed by a Russian civil war. It ended in 1922, with Lenin remaining in power. The country was renamed the Union of Soviet Socialist Republics (USSR).

As 1917 continued, things looked bad for the Allies. With Russia out of the war, Germany hurried to send more men to the Western Front. In spring 1918, they attacked furiously and tried to advance toward Paris. The Allies held them back just long enough for Americans to arrive and help.

By March 1918, 318,000 American soldiers were in France. By August, there were 1.3 million.

At the end of May, the attacking German army was within 56 miles (90 km) of Paris. American divisions were sent into battle. At Belleau Wood, French troops were retreating. The Americans took Belleau Wood from the Germans.

The next major Allied offensive was at Amiens in August. In this well-prepared attack, the Allies retook ground lost over the old Somme battleground. The battle was a major setback for Germany. The Germans' fighting spirit began to break.

A U.S. gun crew operates its weapon during the Meuse-Argonne offensive.

The last major Allied attack of the war was called
Meuse-Argonne. It started with six hours of bombing on
September 26, 1918. Then, more than 700 tanks and Allied

soldiers attacked German positions in the Argonne Forest and along the Meuse River. The battlefield was covered with mud and splintered trees from four years of shelling and battle.

Meuse-Argonne was the largest U.S.-led attack of the war. More than 17,000 Americans were killed. But the fresh waves of American troops were more than the German army could handle.

President Wilson did not want to take sides in the war at first. Why wouldn't Wilson want to fight in a war? What did the United States have to lose?

CHAPTER FOUR

ARMISTICE

By the first week of November 1918, Germany was the only Central Power left. The Ottoman Empire signed an armistice on October 30. Austria-Hungary began breaking apart in October.

The German people had little food left. Britain had been preventing ships from getting to Germany. The people were nearing revolution because of the terrible conditions this caused. The German kaiser, or emperor, left Germany and gave up his power.

On November 11, the two sides signed an armistice. Germany did not officially surrender. But it had to leave all occupied lands. It had to turn over all weapons and submarines.

People around the world celebrated Armistice Day. They cheered and hugged returning soldiers. Church bells rang.

Americans hold newspapers with headlines announcing Germany's surrender.

But many thought of friends and loved ones who had died in the war.

Historians estimate that 65 million men fought in the war. Approximately 8.5 million were killed. More than 21 million were wounded. There were 8 million men listed as missing or

The leaders of Britain, Italy, France, and the United States, known as the "Big Four," decided what would be included in the Treaty of Versailles.

taken prisoner. In addition to soldiers, millions of civilians died from hunger or disease.

The Treaty of Versailles officially ended the war. It was signed on June 28, 1919, five years to the day after Archduke Franz Ferdinand was murdered in Sarajevo.

The Allies wrote the treaty with little say from Germany. The treaty took away Germany's colonies, redrew its boundaries, and gave

SHELL SHOCK

The stress of being under fire constantly in the trenches caused many soldiers to have nervous breakdowns. The condition was called shell shock. Some would shake. Others just stared into space. Many soldiers had nightmares and panic attacks for the rest of their lives.

land back to France. The Allies forced Germany to accept responsibility for the war. Germany had to pay billions of dollars for damage done during the war.

The United States became the world's most powerful country after the war. However, many Americans began to think being in the war was a mistake. More than 115,000 American soldiers died in the war. Many wanted to stay out of future European conflicts.

In Germany, many people thought the treaty was too harsh. A new leader named Adolf Hitler came to power by using Germany's anger toward the treaty. He promised to make Germany a powerful country in Europe again. He said Germany should be able to defend itself and get its land back. Less than 20 years later, Hitler's Germany became a threat again. Another world war had to be fought to stop him.

The towns of northern France were badly damaged during the war. Some small towns were never rebuilt. How would you feel if your town disappeared during a war?

TIMELINE

June 28, 1914	A Serbian nationalist murders Archduke Franz Ferdinand.
August 4, 1914	Germany invades Belgium and France.
August 1914	Russia and Germany battle on the Eastern Front.
May 7, 1915	German U-boats sink the *Lusitania*.
February 21– December 18, 1916	The Battle of Verdun is fought to a draw.
July 1– November 18, 1916	The Battle of the Somme is fought to a draw.
April 6, 1917	The United States declares war on Germany.
November 1917	A new Russian government takes over power and Russia leaves the war.
June 1918	American Marines fight in the Battle of Belleau Wood.
August 1918	The Allies force German troops back in the Battle of Amiens.
September– October 1918	The Battle of Meuse-Argonne is the last major Allied offensive of the war.
November 11, 1918	An armistice ends the fighting.
June 28, 1919	The Treaty of Versailles officially ends World War I.

GLOSSARY

ally (AL-eye) An ally is a country that is on the same side during a war. Britain was one ally of France during World War I.

armistice (AHR-mi-stis) An armistice is a temporary agreement to stop a war. Russia and Germany agreed to an armistice in 1917.

draft (draft) The draft is the system that required men in the United States to join the military. Men chosen in the draft in World War I were sent overseas to fight the Central Powers.

nationalist (NASH-uh-nuh-list) A nationalist wants his or her country to be independent. Gavrilo Princip was a Serbian nationalist.

neutral (NOO-truhl) A neutral country does not support either side in a war. Belgium was neutral in World War I until Germany invaded it.

rationing (RASH-uh-ning) Giving out food in limited amounts is rationing. The United States was able to avoid rationing by having its citizens grow their own vegetables.

shell (shel) A shell is a small bomb that is fired from a cannon. Mustard gas could be fired in a shell.

stalemate (STALE-mate) A stalemate is a situation that results in no progress being made. Trench warfare resulted in a stalemate on the Western Front.

treaty (TREE-tee) A treaty is a formal written agreement between countries. The Treaty of Versailles officially ended World War I.

trenches (TRENCH-iz) Trenches are long, narrow ditches used to protect soldiers in battle. The use of trenches made it difficult for either side to make much progress in the war.

TO LEARN MORE

BOOKS

Samuels, Charlie. *Timeline of World War I.*
New York: Gareth Stevens, 2012.

Walker, Robert. *World War I, 1917–1918: The Turning of the Tide.*
New York: Crabtree, 2014.

WEB SITES

Visit our Web site for links about World War I: **childsworld.com/links**

Note to Parents, Teachers, and Librarians: We routinely verify our Web links to make sure
they are safe and active sites. So encourage your readers to check them out!

INDEX